Nicky and the Big, Bad Wolves

Valeri Gorbachev

North-South Books · New York · London

For Marc Cheshire

Published in the United States by North-South Books Inc., New York.

Published simultaneously in Great Britain, Canada, Australia, and
New Zealand in 1998 by North-South Books, an imprint of
Nord-Süd Verlag AG, Gossau Zürich, Switzerland.

Library of Congress Cataloging-in-Publication Data is available.
A CIP catalogue record for this book is available from The British Library.

The artwork consists of pen-and-ink and watercolor
Designed by Marc Cheshire

ISBN 1-55858-917-1 (TRADE BINDING) 10 9 8 7 6 5 4 3 2 1
ISBN 1-55858-918-X (LIBRARY BINDING) 10 9 8 7 6 5 4 3 2 1
Printed in Belgium

One windy night, Nicky woke up . . .

Mother rushed right in.
"What on earth is the matter?" she asked.

"Wolves!" said Nicky. "A hundred wolves were chasing me!"

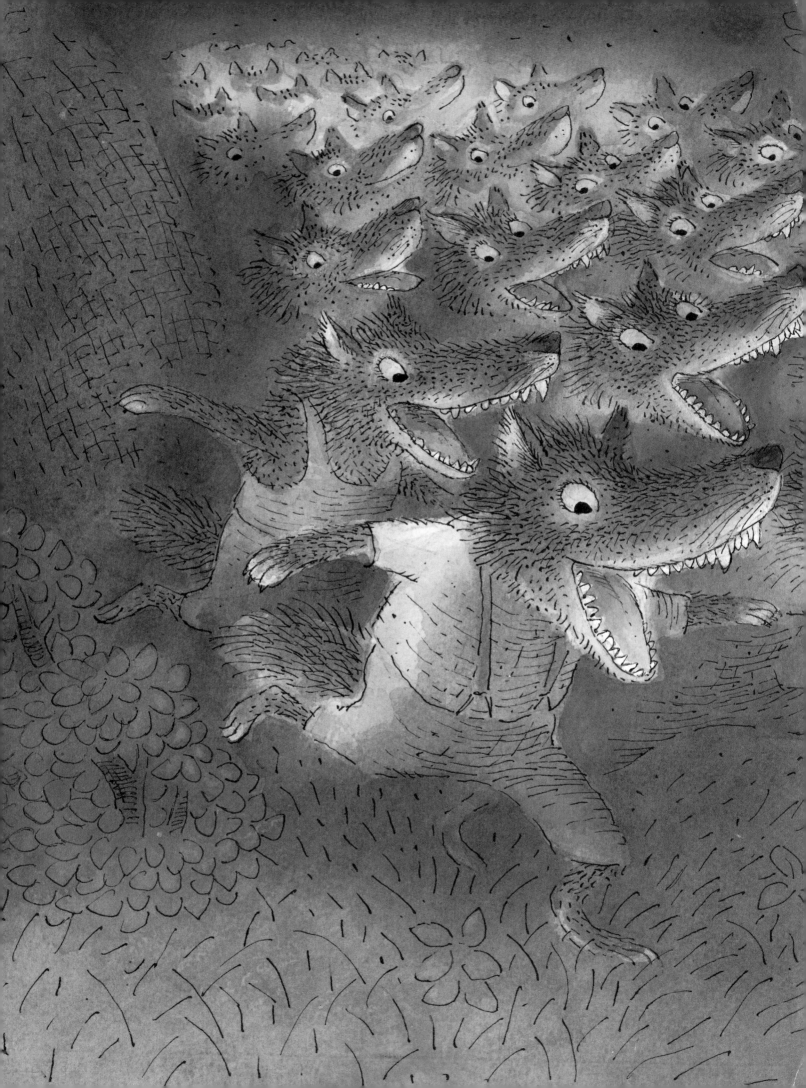

"A *hundred* wolves?" said Mother.
"Are you sure?"

"Well," said Nicky. "Maybe it was *fifty* wolves, but they were racing after me and I couldn't run away fast enough!"

"*Fifty* wolves?" said Mother. "Are you sure?"

"Well," said Nicky. "Maybe it was only *fifteen* wolves, but they were a bloodthirsty bunch."

"Fifteen wolves seems like a lot,"
said Mother. "Are you sure?"

"Well, maybe there were only *five*, actually," admitted Nicky. "But they were right on top of me!"

"It was just a bad dream, Nicky," said Mother. "And now it's time for you all to go back to sleep."

Mother tucked everyone in, turned out the light, and closed the door.

"Did you hear that?" said Nathan.
"It sounded like wolves!" said Nora.
"Hungry wolves!" said Ned.
"With huge fangs," said Nelly.

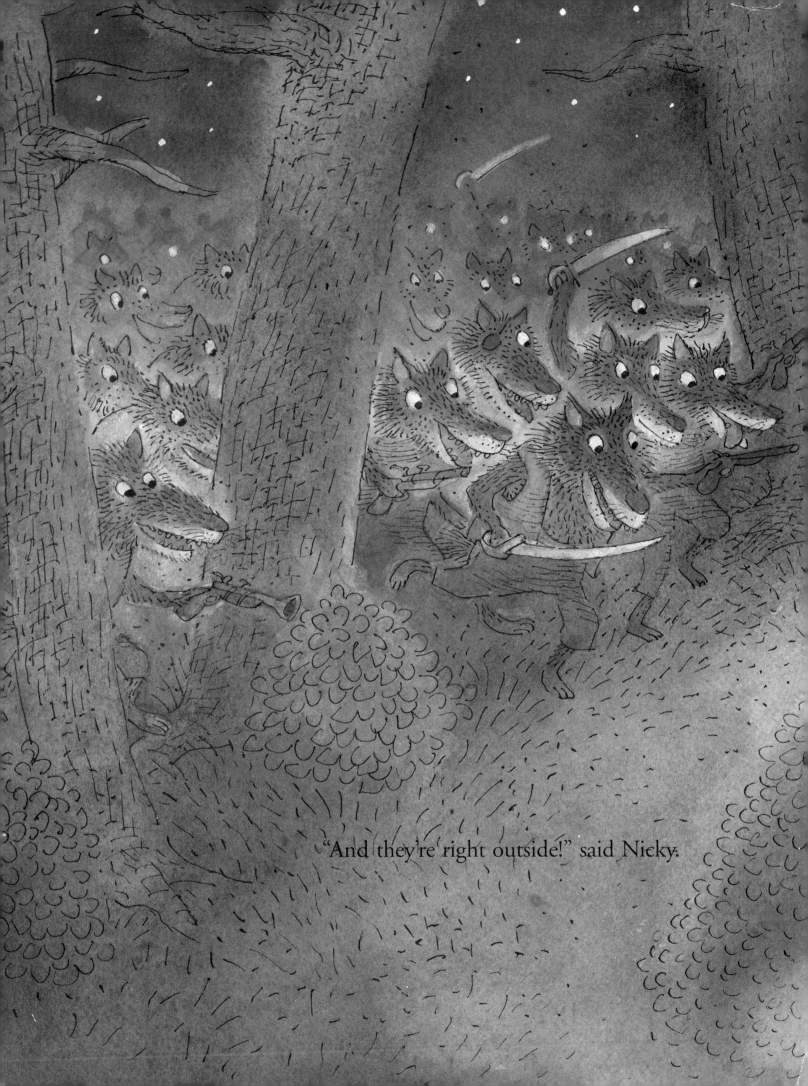

"And they're right outside!" said Nicky.

"*Now* what's the matter?" said Mother.

"A hundred wolves! Right outside our window! They're going to get us!"

"All of you, stay here," said Mother. "I'll settle this wolf business once and for all!"

"There now," said Mother. "Don't worry about those wolves. I chased them all away."

"Are you sure?" said Nicky.

"I'm sure!" said Mother. "But if they come back, I've got my broom right here to chase them away again."

So Nicky and his brothers and sisters all snuggled down and finally went to sleep—with Mother right in the middle!